The Seventh Birthday

By

Bruce E. Arrington

Illustrated By Florence Jayne

Other Birthday Wish books available

The Eighth Birthday Wish

The Ninth Birthday Wish

Visit online at www.pipedreambooks.com.

&OCR&

To my dear family this story is dedicated:

Valerie, who helped with the rhymes;

Hope, who is my inspiration;

Adam, Jessica and Kaylin,

The ultimate cheerleaders.

&OCR&

৪৩৫৪

In a land called Erastus, in faraway space,

Lived a boy in a castle, his home and birthplace.

At the foot of a mountain, oft covered with snow

Was where Wesley, this child, did live and did grow.

৪৩৫৪

Waiting for Seven, a birthday of note,

When a magic door opens, or so it is *hoped*.

For the entrance arrived on the day he turned four,

But was sealed tightly shut, for yet three years more.

But now seven had come, and the sun on that morn,

Kissed Wesley awake, his busy dreams torn.

First, he yawned, and then he stretched.

It was hard to believe, it seemed so farfetched,

That today was the Day, it had come at long last.

There it was—he saw it! A handle to grasp.

☙❦❧

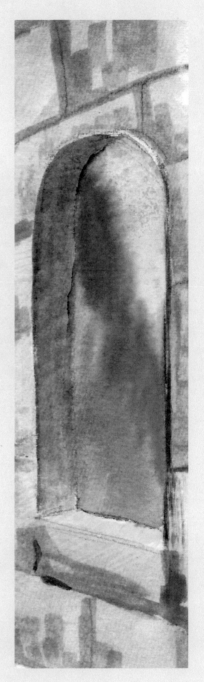

8

He slid off his bed; his feet touched the floor,

He hurried and scurried to that magical door.

And there, right *there*, was a doorknob of gold,

Waiting for Wesley's hand to grab hold.

He grasped it so gently, and turned to the right,

At the sound of a *click* he pulled with his might.

Wesley leaped back, for that large and strong door,

Opened quite quickly with the sound of a roar.

ಜಂಞ

The boy danced in the portal like a crazy old cow,

Until a hand on his shoulder stopped him, right *now*.

There was his mother, with pillow in hand,

Along with a sack lunch, the color of sand.

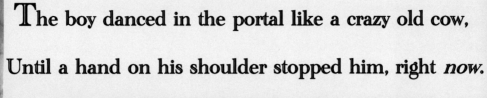

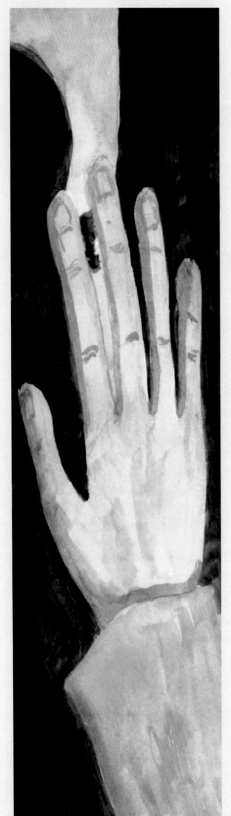

"Breakfast first?" she asked. "It's the start of the day."

But he shook his head gently, and then said "No way,

I'm ready to go and I know what to do,

So please mama, don't start any hull-a-ba-loo."

She winked, and she smiled, and she gave him a nod,

One foot at a time o'er the threshold he trod.

Then he turned and he said, as he looked a bit shy:

"Momma, I know I should hug you goodbye,

But today I'm all grown, so please if you'd try,

To wait and not hug me until I get back,

I'll be just fine, and I'll stay on the track.

My present is waiting, I have only to say,

The thing that I want, and it's mine. So...okay?"

ᘛᗡᘒ

꧁꧂

With a shrug and a twinkle, she blew him a kiss.

He smiled back at her with a heart full of bliss.

The door closed behind him, with a sudden loud boom,

Where light had just been, there was now only gloom.

And for a few seconds his fears from within,

Welled up inside him.

Would they conquer?

Would they win?

꧁꧂

Then excitement surged through him, and he was in awe,

For bright yellow light beamed from cracks, and he saw,

On the ceiling above and on the wall spaces,

High tops and low places: traces

Of doors, tens and hundreds spread over the wall,

With bright beams of light, to dazzle, enthrall.

Their shapes were as varied as their sizes it seemed:

Triangles, circles and big squares that gleamed.

The doors boasted handles, golden and fair,

Yet one door—a round one, was beyond compare.

The handle glowed brightly like none other did,

Wesley chose it at once—that daring, smart kid!

After turning the grip, the door disappeared,

Wesley's heart jumped and he cheered.

A bright sunlit sky, with flowers displayed,

And a grassy green field where he ran and he played.

𝕰𝕺𝕽

Then all around him on a tall, rocky hill,

Wesley spied them, and thrilled, he sat still.

There! Winged horses of lavender, rose and bright green,

A most colorful, wonderful scene.

Black ones, and brown ones and grey ones as well,

Dancing in air as if under some spell.

They were zigging and zagging, some of them swirling.

Then Wesley saw his, she was leaping and twirling.

Her color turned chestnut, then orange, and then blue,

With patterns never seen in a zoo:

Striped ones, and spotted ones, solid ones too.

𝕰𝕺𝕽

ℰↃↅ

*T*his *flyer*, the boy thought, *is too good to be true.*

Yet to Wesley she flew, and landing like dew,

She knelt down beside him, and brave as could be,

He reached out to touch her, and then he could see,

As she fluttered her wings and nibbled his side,

She wanted and hoped he would climb up and glide.

He thought for a second, *Could it be so?*

Should I go?

Did she know that today was *his* day?

That by wishing one wish, he could take her away?

But the mare only neighed as he started to climb,

(Her coat now appearing the color of lime).

ℰↃↅ

Up one side, then the other, fall after fall,

He toppled eight ways, losing balance and all,

'Til a flyer stood beside him, sturdy and tall.

Lifting Wesley straight up by the seat of his pants,

Set him right square—that wasn't by chance.

So with food in the one hand and pillow in the other,

Wesley locked in his legs and thought of his mother.

She wouldn't believe what I'm doing, he thought,

As the horses took off from that very spot.

Wesley laughed loud and long at the wind in his hair,

Where the flyers would take him, well he didn't care!

With arms lifted high, and both eyes closed tight shut,

Feeling rhythm of horse wings down deep in his gut.

He heard someone speak, way up in the breeze,

Like a sigh in the wind, passing through the trees.

"Wesley!" came a voice, that the boy knew quite well,

"Are you having fun? You're looking so swell!"

"Hi momma!" he cried, as he settled right down.

He giggled at her voice, and grinned like a clown,

As he looked all around at hundreds of stars,

All the planets swirling near, especially Mars!

The spinning and humming grew faster and louder,

As the moon winked at Wesley, he never felt prouder

Than being with flyers who sailed through the sky,

And neighed as they soared. But then, by and by,

They flew closer together, straight down it did seem,

Through clouds of white, down slopes of white steam.

So fast they descended right down to the ground,

That Wesley's tummy was sloshed all around.

All his insides were tickled but he only laughed more,

As he slid off his flyer, and began to explore.

All around him, a colorful farm he did see,

With thousands of sunflowers, big as a tree,

Red, orange, yellow, and even light pea.

෫⃝ⓒ⃝

A black flyer stood in a tiny corral,

Near a pathway lined with green chaparral.

A single white star shone on his forehead,

With a tall dark body, he looked very well bred.

The flyers ran and stood outside his small fence,

And Wesley noticed they started to tense.

Some of them neighed or pawed at the ground,

The black flyer, it seemed, could not come 'round.

And then Wesley heard a slamming-door sound.

From a house came a teen with a leap and bound.

His eyes—they were brown and his hair was too.

He clapped his hands, whistled, and then he threw

His hat in the air, and he shouted, "Flying horses!"

Then looking at Wesley he cried, "Let's join forces!

We'll catch them and then we can fly them all day,

We'll feed them well from my barn filled with hay!"

The teen ran toward them, but the flyers took off.

He then looked at Wesley with an obvious scoff.

"Didn't you bring all those flyers for me?"

Wesley shook his head, saying, "Why do I see

A captive horse instead of one free?

Is he hurt? Can't he fly? Has he nowhere to go?"

℘℘℘

ℰℴℛ

The other boy looked and then jeered, "Hello?

His name is Starnight, and he is *my* horse,

I think you should have known that, of course!"

"Did he pick *you*?" Wesley asked, thinking quick.

The other shook his head as he picked up a stick.

"It was my birthday," he said. "So I picked *him*.

He's only a horse. Are you *that* dim?"

Looking at the flyers, those marvelous creatures,

Wesley considered all their fabulous features.

ℛℴℰ

Their love for each other, their grace, their care,

And now their friend, Starnight, without a prayer,

Couldn't be free, or with his family so dear.

And so, with that thought, Wesley walked near.

And he said, "He needs to go free."

"Why?" the teen asked. "I sure disagree!"

"But it's *my* birthday now," Wesley said,

As he stared at the horses and their faces of dread.

"I want Starnight to go back to his family,"

Wesley wished firmly, without hint of a plea.

Like magic the ropes dropped away from the horse,

But Starnight stood waiting, with no use of force,

To escape from that place, though he now had the choice.

Wesley looked at the tall boy, whose face was fraught,

With struggles inside, though likely as not,

Wesley guessed he would fight, against Starnight's will,

To trap him somehow, to keep him yet still.

But as soon as the teen walked up to that gate,

Wesley held up his hand, and shouted, "Wait!

Before you decide and throw it away,

Could you ask him? Would he let you, join in the play?"

He slowly walked up to Starnight that day,

"I guess you are free to go on your way."

The horse nuzzled his shoulder and put up his ears,

As the boy looked hopeful, in spite of his fears.

"I don't have to push or forcefully guide?

I just have to ask, and let you decide."

ଌର

30

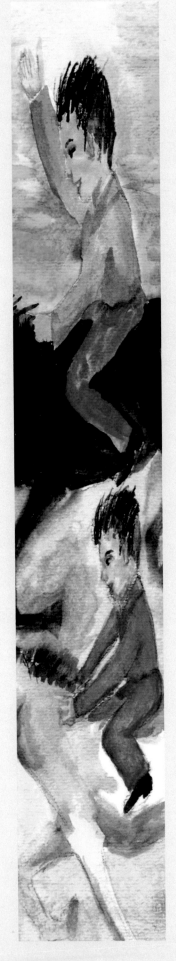

Starnight bumped his shoulder, the boy staggered back

With a grin on his face, "Hey! Cut me some slack!"

The teen turned to Wesley, "I guess Mom was right,

Sometimes you don't have to use all your might.

Want to go for a ride?" he asked, his voice sounding freed,

Suddenly delivered from his habit of greed.

Wesley nodded and smiled. "Sure, you can lead."

For hours that day they played and climbed trees,

Even raced a few flyers, remembering, "Please?"

The horses were grateful for Wesley's good deed,

Knowing he could have been taken with greed,

And kept for himself a fine flying steed.

☙❦☙

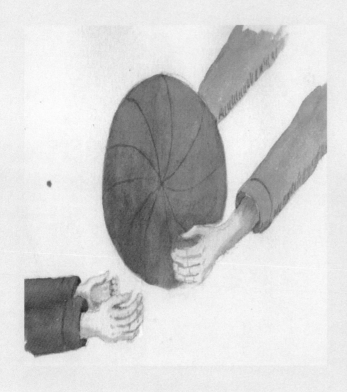

At the end of the day, Wesley waved *bye* to his friend,

And somehow he knew that this wasn't the end.

He climbed on the mare for one final ride,

Then settled right down and curled on his side.

ℰ∞ℂ

With his head on his pillow and not the least grim,

He smoothed her sleek side, as the daylight grew dim.

His birthday was past; his wish had come true,

His gifts received had been more than a few.

Well the next thing he knew, Wesley fell fast asleep

And when he awoke, he found darkness so deep.

But he knew where he was: in the Room with the Doors,

Only one light remained, from his room near the floor.

಼ೂೞ

35

ଛଠଔଓ

Wesley ran toward the glow, a smile on his face,

The Door opened, with bright light in its place.

There was his mother, with arms open wide,

Wesley hugged her, kissed her, and happily cried.

"Know what, momma?" he asked with eyes full of play,

"You'll never believe what I have to say!"

The End

ଛଠଔଓ

About the Author

Bruce Arrington spent much of his childhood tromping through the woods and streams of Hood River Valley, Oregon. After completing his schooling at Oregon State University, he worked as a wildlife biologist in Oregon's old growth forests and south Florida's Everglades swamps.

Looking for even more adventure, Bruce changed careers and became a teacher in the historic, small town of Paisley, Oregon. He lives there with his wife, Hope, three venturesome teens, and several spoiled pets.

Visit online at www.pipedreambooks.com

About the Artist

Florence Jayne, of Paisley Oregon, is the illustrator for The Seventh Birthday Wish. She brings many years of artistic talent and enthusiasm into the school art classroom.

Made in the USA
Lexington, KY
05 November 2018